S. N. BOSE

S. N. BOSE

THE IMMORTAL SCIENTIST

Dilip M. Salwi

Revised Edition

RUPA

Published by
Rupa Publications India Pvt. Ltd. 2015
7/16, Ansari Road, Daryaganj
New Delhi 110002

Sales centres:
Allahabad   Bengaluru   Chennai
Hyderabad   Jaipur   Kathmandu
Kolkata   Mumbai

Photographs courtesy: S. N. Bose National Centre
for Basic Science, Kolkata

The views and opinions expressed in this book are the author's own and
the facts are as reported by him which have been verified to the extent
possible, and the publishers are not in any way liable for the same.

ISBN: 978-81-291-3675-6

First impression 2015

10 9 8 7 6 5 4 3 2 1

The moral right of the author has been asserted.

Typeset by Ninestars Information Technologies Ltd, Chennai

To a friend and well-wisher,
Prof Suresh C. Garg,
for his commitment to
scientific research and science education

CONTENTS

CHAPTER ONE

IMMORTALITY AT ONE STROKE

In the early 1920s, a new university was established at Dhaka, (now in Bangladesh). A young lecturer from Calcutta University was appointed to the higher post of Reader in its Department of Physics. To the astonishment of the young man, a chaotic environment then prevailed in the department. While the old, classical physics curriculum was being rather casually taught to the students, the physics laboratory was in utter disorder. The young man however did not lose heart and began to organise the department and its laboratory. He also began to teach the then newly emerging subject of modern physics to the post-graduate students.

Earlier, at Calcutta University, the young man had learnt modern physics on his own after learning German.

Max Planck and Niels Bohr (top to bottom)

He and his former classmate, colleague and friend Meghnad Saha had read the latest books on modern physics in German that they had borrowed from a German physics teacher, P. J. Bruhl of Sibpur Engineering College. In fact, the two friends had also translated Albert Einstein's famous Theory of Relativity from German into English for the first time in the world. They had also started teaching the latest developments in modern physics, like Max Planck's Quantum Theory, Niels Bohr's Atomic Theory and Albert Einstein's Theory of Relativity to their students and had begun to conduct research in it. He and Saha had jointly written a research paper on a modern physics topic which had appeared in a British science journal. Subsequently, he had also written two more research papers in mathematics.

Albert Einstein

While his work at the physics laboratory and teaching continued, the young man was also planning to conduct research in modern physics. During his spare time he would go through the original papers of eminent physicists like Niels Bohr, Arnold Sommerfeld and Willard Gibbs. Then he read Max Planck's classic book *Heat and Thermodynamics* which one of his former friends had brought as a gift from Europe. But his research studies continued in complete intellectual isolation as there was nobody available in the Department with whom he could discuss his work or his growing interest in modern physics.

With classmate, colleague and friend Meghnad

The real stimulus for research however came in April 1924 when the young man invited Meghnad Saha, who was then a Professor of Physics at Allahabad University, to Dhaka. Saha had already gained international recognition for his wonderful formula in astrophysics. He came to Dhaka University to take the practical examination of M.Sc. students. After the examination, Saha sat with him over tea and snacks in his room to discuss things of mutual interest—teaching and research in modern physics.

In due course, the discussion shifted to the problems they both faced while teaching the most significant formula concerning heat radiation forwarded by the German physicist Max Planck because it contained some logical inconsistencies and ad hoc assumptions. Then Saha told his young friend to look up a specific research paper in which there was, what he called 'some crazy idea'. In fact, he left a copy of that paper and a few others with the young man.

After Saha left Dhaka, the young man went through the papers carefully. Indeed, what Saha had remarked was absolutely true. The paper contained a crazy idea which he himself could not digest. He therefore decided to dig into the subject right from its fundamentals because as a perfectionist he never accepted an idea unless he himself was satisfied.

Quite soon, he faced the logical inconsistencies and ad hoc assumptions that Planck had used in obtaining his important formula. He now endeavoured to obtain the same formula after removing the inconsistencies and cutting down those assumptions. He spent several sleepless nights mulling over this difficult problem.

Finally, through a combination of logic and imagination he introduced some novel concepts and ideas and obtained the same formula successfully. However, he had no idea of the significance of the extraordinary

Bose's research paper in his handwriting

contribution that he had made. All he knew was that he had conceived something which was worth writing down as a research paper. He wrote a short, four page research paper on what he had accomplished and sent it to the British science journal *The Philosophical Magazine*, which had earlier published one of his papers.

When the journal did not respond, the young man took the bold step of sending his paper directly to none other than Albert Einstein—the most eminent and famous physicist alive in the world then. He hoped the paper would be published in a prestigious German science journal. He had thought of Einstein because the great physicist had himself tried to solve this problem without success. Moreover, Einstein had earlier graciously given him and Saha the permission to translate and publish his famous *Theory of Relativity* into English.

One look at the paper convinced Einstein of the originality of the concepts and ideas forwarded by the young Indian. Impressed, he himself translated the short paper into German immediately and sent it for publication in the reputed physics journal *Zeitchrift fur Physik*. He also added a remark at the end: '...an important step forward'. The paper was duly published in the September 1924 issue of the journal. It created a big stir among physicists in Europe and led to rapid developments in modern physics. Overnight, our young Indian scientist, who was then hardly 30, became a familiar name to all the physicists of the world. And not simply that, in due course, his name became immortal in the history of physics—half the elementary particles in the universe are today named after him. His work has also become one of the central columns supporting the edifice of modern physics.

Today, a class of elementary particles is named 'Bosons', a type of statistics is named 'Bose-Einstein Statistics' and an unusual state of matter is named 'Bose-Einstein Condensation' after him. In recent times, this unusual state of matter has also been created in the laboratory. In the decades to come, no text-book on modern physics can be written without mentioning his name. That young man was Satyendranath Bose, more popularly known as 'Satyen Bose.'

This amazing work of Bose—essentially a big leap of imagination about matter and radiation—illustrates how a person can make a fundamental contribution to science by not taking anything for granted and investigating a subject from its foundations.

CHAPTER TWO

THE LONELY RESEARCHER

Satyendranath Bose was a New Year gift to Indian science as he was born on January 1, 1894 in an educated, middle class family of Kolkata. It was a typical 'Bhadralok' family of respectable, white collar workers. Not only his father but even his grandfather had served in the British Administration and the family was open to western ideas and thoughts. Bose's mother too came from a family of lawyers. The family belonged originally to the fairly prosperous village of Bara Jajuli, about 48 kilometres from Kolkata, in the Nadia district of West Bengal. Before Kolkata gained prominence as a city, Bara Jajuli was a centre of cultural and intellectual activities.

The family was undergoing a financial crisis at the time Bose was born. Settled in Kolkata for two

Young Bose

generations, Bose's father owned an ancestral house in the city but it was occupied by tenants when Bose was born. So he spent his childhood in a rented accommodation. At that stage, his father, Surendra Nath Bose, was employed as an accountant in the British East India Railways and was posted in Assam and North Bengal.

Bose was the only son in the family as he was followed by six sisters. When anybody teased his mother she always retorted smilingly, 'I would rather bear a dozen daughters than another son who is not worthy of being a brother to Satyen.' Called by the nickname 'Bodi', he was studious, mischievous and social. He savoured every aspect of life—eating 'sandesh', making friends, playing carrom and chess, walking in the rain, and asking curious questions, such as, what is the difference between rain water and tap water? Is it possible to stop ageing? and so on. He was a restless, curious child who always wanted to know more. To keep him off mischief, his disciplinarian father used to dictate questions

The family house where Bose was born

on mathematics that Bose would scribble with chalk on the floor of a store room. On his return from office, he would check whether his son had solved the problems correctly or not.

Throughout his school days, Bose came first in his class and he did particularly well in mathematics. His mathematics teacher, Upendranath Bakshi, was very proud of him and was convinced his student would one day follow the footsteps of great mathematicians like Pierre Simon Laplace and Augustin Louis Cauchy. Once he even gave Bose 110 out of 100 marks! When Bose's father wanted to know if it was a mistake, the teacher laughed and told him that he gave more marks because Bose had also attempted the alternate questions and answered correctly. Later, his college mathematics teacher also gave him full marks when he solved the questions in more than one way. Even his British college teacher, who taught him English, used to call young Bose a 'genius'.

Father, Surendra Nath Bose and mother, Amodini Bose

In one respect, however, Bose was different from the other brilliant and studious boys often found in schools and colleges. He never kept his knowledge and abilities to himself but tried his best to share them with his friends and classmates. In fact, he would often coach his classmates in mathematics after school hours. This generosity and absence of arrogance is an exceedingly rare trait—often not found in men of genius. And this characteristic would remain his hallmark throughout life. Later, it made him very popular among his students, colleagues and fellow scientists.

During his early education at New Indian School and Hindu School, Bose was keen on scientific experiments, though as a subject it was not taught to him. Once he built a telescope and on another occasion an electric

Bose playing the Esraj

battery. He also produced coal gas by heating coal in a closed container. In these exploratory ventures, his neighbourhood friends, Pashupati and Girjapati Bhattacharya, were his helpmates. Bose spent most of his free time in their home.

The Bhattacharyas were an intellectual, cultured and music-loving family and they had a library where he could delve into the world of books. In the company of the Bhattacharyas, Bose's interest in music grew and he learnt to play the musical instrument called 'Esraj' and even began to compose 'ragas'. Later, in spite of a ban by his father, he and his friends would also secretly attend musical concerts.

Meanwhile, in 1905, the Partition of Bengal had triggered off passionate protests all across Bengal. At street corners of Kolkata, meetings, mass rallies and bonfires of British goods were organised as a protest against the Partition. It had a lasting impact on the impressionable mind of young Bose. In an answer to a call by the poet

Seated (left to right): P. B. Sarkar, Amaresh Chakravarty, P. C. Ray, T. S. Muttu, S. N. Bose. Standing (left to right): M. N. Saha, U. N. Karmakar, J. C. Ghosh, J. N. Mukherjee

Rabindranath Tagore no food was cooked at Bose's home on the festive day of 'Rakshabandhan'.

At a time when even matchboxes were imported into India, the Swadeshi movement triggered off the spirit of self-reliance in Bengal. In fact, his father was so enthused by the Swadeshi movement that he gave up the accountant's job. In 1901, he started a chemical factory, called Indian Chemicals and Pharmaceutical Works, almost at the same time as the great Indian chemist P. C. Ray set up his pioneering chemical industry in Bengal.

In those turbulent days, Bose and his friends would visit Cornwallis Square, now known as Azad Hind Bagh, and sing patriotic songs composed by Tagore. He had had also became a member of *Anushilan Samiti,* a secret society, which gave lessons on physical fitness and handling of weapons and many Indian revolutionaries belonged to the society. He had also begun to conduct night classes to teach underprivileged children. These night schools were later banned by the British rulers because they were suspected to have become bomb-making factories. In his college there were several students who were revolutionaries but Bose never mixed with them because his father had given him strict instructions not to do so. He did not openly join their activities but later helped them indirectly by giving them shelter and acting as a courier to carry their money. He did this even when he was abroad.

Bose was a voracious reader and his favourites were poets like Alfred Tennyson, Tagore and Kalidasa. He knew Kalidasa's *Meghdoot* and Tennyson's *In Memoriam* by heart. Later, when he learnt French and German, he enjoyed the works of Victor Hugo and Johann Wolfgang von Goethe. He even tried his hand at creative writing when he and his friends brought out a hand-written magazine called *Manisha* (Intellect) which survived only a few issues. In the magazine, he wrote of his childhood experiences when he used to accompany his father to the picturesque hills and tea gardens of Assam.

Seated (left to right): M. N. Saha, J. C. Bose, J. C. Ghosh. Standing (left to right): Snehamoy Dutt, S. N. Bose, N. R. Sen, J. N. Mukherjee, N. C. Nag

Bose had also become a part of a literary group called *Sabuj Patra* (The Green Leaf) which met every week in the evenings to discuss and debate on various subjects, especially Bengali literature and its new trends. Some contemporary literary giants, including members of the Tagore family belonged to the group. Later when he went to Dhaka, Bose joined a similar group called *Baaro Jana* (The Twelve). In short, Bose led a social life full of nationalistic fervour flavoured with literature, poetry and music. These varied interests stuck to him throughout his life.

No. 1

CALCUTTA UNIVERSITY.

M. Sc. Marks.

The following are the marks obtained by *Satyendra Nath Bose*

No. 1 *Presidency* College at the M. Sc. Examination 1915

in *Mixed Mathematics*

	Theoretical.									
	First Paper.	Second Paper.	Third Paper.	Fourth Paper.	Fifth Paper.	Sixth Paper.	Seventh Paper.	Eighth Paper.	Total.	Grand Total.
	98	85	100	89	88	94	98	84	736	

SENATE HOUSE.

The 15.9.1915.

P. Brühl
Registrar,

Bose's M.Sc. certificate showing his record-setting marks

In the meanwhile, Bose had entered Presidency College after doing brilliantly in the school leaving examinations. At Presidency he had teachers like the scientist J. C. Bose, who had invented wireless telegraphy and showed that plants have feelings, and P. C. Ray, who was a renowned chemist, industrialist and social worker. While J. C. Bose was rather withdrawn, always busy with his experiments and difficult to interact with, Ray was much more accessible and always made his lectures interesting by sprinkling them with anecdotes about great scientists. Ray had considerable influence on Bose as he espoused the Swadeshi cause. Although he never mixed with revolutionaries in college, he once addressed

Bose's wife, Ushabati

a protest meeting against a British teacher who had made a derogatory remark— 'Don't chatter like monkeys' — against Indians but had later apologized. P. C. Mahalnobis, Nilratan Dhar and S. K. Mitra, who later made a mark in Indian science, were all senior to him.

Meghnad Saha joined his class when Bose was doing his post-graduation in mixed mathematics, what is today known as 'Mathematical Physics'. Although Bose and Saha were both brilliant students and always competed for the first position in the class, the competition was always healthy. They were good friends and their friendship lasted till the end of their lives. In 1915, Bose passed M.Sc. examination in the first position with Saha following him with the second. For standing first, he received the Hemchandra Gossain Prize and Gold Medal. In fact, he secured record marks in M.Sc. which have yet to be surpassed in the history of Calcutta University!

After finishing M.Sc. Bose was keen to take up a job because he had a family to look after. He had married Ushabati in 1914 when he was barely twenty years old.

Ushabati's father was a well-to-do doctor in Kolkata who saw Bose on one of his visits to Bose's house. He was impressed by the good-looking boy who was also doing very well in studies. He put forward the proposal of marriage to Bose's mother, who readily agreed after seeing the 11-year-old Ushabati. Somehow Bose did not object to the marriage as he wanted to see his mother happy but he turned down the dowry. Thus he took on family responsibilities at a very early age. In the early days of marriage, he used to teach Ushabati English because she had had only primary education.

In those days in Kolkata or for that matter, in India—jobs involving science were scarce. Fellowships for research were also not available. What was worse, due to his high qualifications Bose was rejected twice. Both the Bihar Government and Alipore Meteorological Office found him 'overqualified' for jobs. When his father suggested that he should try for a job in the East India Railways, he showed no interest. When once he applied for a fellowship to study abroad, he was again disqualified—this time his marriage stood in the way. The fellowship was not offered to married candidates because it was feared that they would spend money on their wives rather than on books and equipment. Disappointed, Bose continued, like Saha, to make ends meet by taking private tuitions.

Ashutosh Mukherjee, the 'Tiger' of Bengal

It was during a meeting with Saha that the two decided to meet the then Vice Chancellor of Calcutta University, Ashutosh Mukherjee, the 'Tiger' of Bengal. Through the grapevine they had heard that he was planning to establish a new college of science and was looking for teaching staff. With considerable courage they decided to meet him to find out if any openings existed for fresh science post-graduates.

Mukherjee had already heard of the brilliance of both Saha and Bose. When he came to know the reason for their meeting, he asked them what could they teach. In enthusiasm, the two blurted out, 'Anything, Sir!' Mukherjee laughed and offered them lectureships on a meagre salary in the Department of Applied Mathematics, at the newly set up University College of Science. Both the young men were jubilant at this unexpected turn of events.

Thus, in 1916, began the careers of two great Indian physicists. But, quite soon both found it difficult to work under the Head of the Department, Ganesh Prasad, a foreign-returned mathematician, who had the habit of running down the other teachers. Bose always believed in plain speaking and once told Prasad not to criticize the teachers for the bad performance of the students because he himself set very difficult question papers. Prasad was annoyed and remarked that Bose might be good in studies but he was not cut out for research! When Bose and Saha could not work with Prasad any more, Ashutosh Mukherjee transferred them to the newly set up of Department of Physics. Of course, he was unsure of the managerial capabilities of two inexperienced lecturers fresh out of college. They had the responsibility of setting up Department from scratch. They had to not only teach physics but also to set the curriculum, courses and establish a laboratory.

Both the young men turned out to be much more enthusiastic and ambitious than Mukherjee had expected. They were not simply interested in teaching physics but also work on the emerging field of 'modern' physics. In those days physics was being revolutionised by new concepts and ideas, such as Max Planck's Quantum Theory which claimed that energy is released or absorbed in the form of small packets, called 'quanta'; Niels Bohr's Atomic Theory which claimed that the inside of the atom was like the solar system; and Albert Einstein's Theory of

Relativity which radically changed the concept of space and time. Both Saha and Bose were keen to learn these new theories and concepts and also to teach them to their students. Besides, they also fervently hoped to do research in the frontiers of modern physics.

However, when the two young men searched for the latest books on modern physics in the college library there were none. Then at the suggestion of Mukherjee, they began to search for books in the libraries of neighbouring colleges. Finally, they could obtain the requisite books from the library of a German named P. J. Bruhl, who was teaching physics at the neighbouring Shibpur Engineering College. But then they discovered that all the books were in the German language.

Saha already knew German because he had learnt it during graduation. Bose had however taken French classes from a French lady as he was fond of reading French literature. Now with great enthusiasm he began to learn German. While Saha concentrated on subjects like 'Thermodynamics'—the science of heat, and 'Spectroscopy'—the study of sunlight and starlight, Bose took upon himself the task of learning the theories of 'Electromagnetism'—the study of interaction between electricity and magnetism, and the Theory of Relativity.

In 1919, Albert Einstein and his Theory of Relativity became famous all over the world when the total solar eclipse in Africa confirmed his prediction that the light

Albert Einstein

coming from stars is bent by a massive body, such as, the sun. Everybody was keen to know not only about Einstein but also to understand his theory. Among the few Indian physicists who knew and understood the theory were Saha and Bose. Saha therefore wrote

S. N. Bose

articles in both English and Bengali newspapers giving a popular version of the theory. In fact, interest in the theory was so high among physics students in Kolkata colleges that they became keen to read the original papers of Einstein.

It then struck Saha and Bose that it would be a good idea to translate Einstein's theory from German into English. They sent a letter to Einstein requesting permission to translate his original papers into English and also publish them. Although Einstein had some problems with his English publishers, he immediately gave the necessary permission for translation into English for circulation in India only. As it turned out, Saha and Bose's translation and subsequent publication of *The Principles of Relativity* in 1919 by Calcutta University was the first English version of Einstein's highly acclaimed theory in the world.

Meanwhile, Saha and Bose had not only started teaching modern physics but had also began to conduct research on it. Although there was nobody to guide them, no peers to discuss the subject except themselves and no up to date library to cater to their needs, they jointly wrote a research paper in 1918. This was the only research paper ever written jointly by two giants of Indian science. Subsequently, both Saha and Bose went separate ways as their areas of specialisation were different. Saha became fascinated by astrophysics, wrote some classic research papers and went abroad for further studies. Bose wrote two more papers in mathematics which were published locally.

After his good friend and research collaborator Saha left on a fellowship for Europe, Bose felt even more isolated in the Department. He had no peers to discuss the latest developments in modern physics. Moreover, his plain speaking had brought him trouble. It all began when Ashutosh Mukherjee found that students did not attempt one particular question he had set for two or three successive years and he blamed the teachers for not teaching mathematics properly.

At the teacher's meeting, Bose confronted Mukherjee openly and told him in plain terms that it did not reflect upon their teaching but that the question itself was wrongly set by Mukherjee. Although Mukherjee was generous enough to admit his mistake openly, it spoiled their relationship and thereafter Bose could not establish any rapport with him. Besides, he found that C. V. Raman who had joined the college as Khaira Professor of Physics was attracting a large number of research students from all over the country. There was always much competition for equipment, manpower and resources among the researchers leading to a lot of ill will. Finally Bose decided to quit and began to look for a job elsewhere.

CHAPTER THREE

FLASH OF A GENIUS

After the Partition of Bengal in 1905, the British Government established the Dhaka University to placate the East Bengalis. Its first Vice Chancellor Phillip Hartog was searching for a suitable candidate for the post of Reader in Physics. He came to know about Bose's experience in organising the curriculum, courses and laboratory at the Calcutta University and offered him the post. Bose readily agreed to join the Dhaka University at the higher post of a Reader.

In 1921, when he arrived at Dhaka University, he found the entire Physics Department in a highly disorganised state. Teaching of physics was somehow in progress but the laboratory was in chaos. So he decided to first organise the Department before venturing to do any research.

Dhaka University

When his friend D. M. Bose had returned from Germany two years earlier, he had presented him a copy of Max Planck's classic book *Heat and Thermodynamics*. Bose had gone through the book carefully but was not satisfied with the way Planck had obtained his famous formula for radiation. He felt that it contained some ad hoc assumptions taken to suit the requirements and therefore needed further scrutiny. It was however Meghnad Saha, as narrated in the beginning of this book, who actually provoked him to re-examine the formula. This set him on to the path of a major discovery, whose significance even Bose himself did not realise when he wrote the research paper. What was that fundamental discovery which has today made him immortal in the annals of physics?

It is not easy to explain the scientific discovery made by Bose because, for one, it involves complicated mathematics and, secondly, the subject is highly abstract. Yet it is of fundamental value to modern physics. A flavour of his discovery, with the relevant perspective, is given below.

What is physics? It deals with matter and energy and the interactions between them. The various forms of energy that everybody is familiar with are heat, light and electricity. Modern physics focusses on the internal structure of matter and the interactions between energy and elementary particles of matter taking place inside the atom. It was while studying radiations, the energy emitted by a source of heat, that in 1900 the great German physicist Max Planck arrived at the revolutionary theory, called 'Quantum theory'. The theory was that energy is emitted or absorbed in small packets, called 'quanta' (in German, quantum means 'small packet').

Using this theory, Planck also obtained mathematically the crucial formula that successfully explained the distribution of energy emitted by a black body, an 'ideal' source of heat, which perfectly agreed with its experimental measurements. Earlier, several other eminent physicists, such as, Wilhelm Wien, Lord Rayleigh and James Jeans had also tried to obtain an experimentally verifiable formula using conventional or 'classical' ideas but were not fully successful. Planck's Quantum Theory therefore emerged a winner in explaining the way energy is emitted or absorbed. It was therefore hailed as a major milestone and laid the foundation of modern physics.

The three decades—1900 to 1930—that followed Planck's theory were years of tumultuous developments in physics. Its classical foundation was literally shaken. New ideas about the internal structure of the atom, wave-particle duality of matter, the concepts of space and time etc. were emerging. In short, perceptions about matter and energy were fast changing. Bose's paper made a timely appearance at this crucial juncture.

It was not only he and Saha but also several eminent European physicists who were not satisfied with Planck's mathematical derivation of the formula. Planck had resorted to some ad hoc assumptions and logical inconsistencies to match the formula with his experimental findings. Even Einstein had tried his hand at setting things right but without much success. For want of a better method of derivation of the formula, Planck's method was accepted for the time being. Such compromises between mathematics and experimental results may sound odd but it is a common practice in science.

American physicist Arthur Compton

When Bose began to re-examine Planck's formula, he was not very well acquainted with 'Statistical Mechanics'. It is a powerful mathematical tool required to calculate the macroscopic behaviour of an assembly of particles from their microscopic properties. In making mathematical calculations about energy or radiation emitted by a black body, acquaintance with this tool was therefore a must. But Bose had the remarkable ability of not taking things for granted. He firmly believed that one should 'Never accept an idea as long as you yourself are not satisfied'. He decided to re-do the mathematical calculations on the basis of the latest scientific findings. Earlier, Einstein had shown the particle nature of light through his newly propounded 'photoelectric Effect'. But it was the American physicist Arthur Compton who, by discovering the 'Compton Effect', had conclusively shown that light also behaves like particles, though it was not yet named 'photon'.

In short, Bose started from scratch with a fresh and open mind, without the biases of eminent European physicists. He also made several assumptions to derive the formula. Surprisingly, all those intuitively made assumptions about elementary particles, namely, light-quanta or photons, proved later to be absolutely correct. And, to his own satisfaction, he could mathematically obtain Planck's formula accurately. It was a triumph of imagination and intuition—the two powerful tools of exploration of ancient Indian sages.

When Bose wrote down his findings in the form of a research paper, they covered a mere four pages! At that

PHYSICS DEPARTMENT,
Dacca University.

Dacca, the _4th June_ 1924.

Respected Sir,
I have ventured to lend you the accompanying article for your perusal and opinion. I am anxious to know what you think of it. You will be that (I have tried to deduce the coefficient $\frac{8\pi\nu^2}{c^3}$ in Planck's Law independent of the classical electrodynamics,) only assuming that the ultimate elementary regions in the Phase-space has the content h^3) I do not have sufficient german to translate the paper. If you think the paper worth publication. I shall be grateful if you arrange for its publication in Zeitschrift für Physik. Though a complete stranger to you, I do not feel any hesitation in making such a request. Because we are all your pupils though profiting only by your teachings through your writings. I don't know whether you still remember that some body from Calcutta asked your permission to translate your papers on Relativity in English. You acceded to the request, the book has since been published. I was the one who translated your paper on Generalised Relativity.

Yours faithfully,
S. N. Bose

Bose's letter of 4th June, 1924 to Einstein

stage, he did not realise the wider implications of his assumptions about photons. In fact he never thought he had done anything novel. It was simply 'his way' of looking at radiation. As it turned out, his attempt was not merely a self-contained method of obtaining the formula correctly, but a conceptually novel way of looking at matter and energy.

Bose first sent a copy of the paper 'Planck's Law and Light Quantum Hypothesis' to the British science journal *Philosophical Magazine* published in London, U.K., which had earlier published one of his papers. But when he did not receive any response from the journal for some time, he took the bold step of sending the paper directly to Einstein. It was a turning point in Bose's scientific career and life. What would have been the outcome had he sent it to a lesser authority could be anybody's guess!

Addressing Einstein as 'Sir' and calling himself his 'distant pupil' in the tradition of Mahabharata's 'Eklavya', and also referring to the English translation of the Theory of Relativity, Bose enclosed the small paper for the great physicist's scrutiny. He hoped for a possible translation into German for publication in the journal *Zeitschrift fuer Physik*, if found suitable. Indeed, it was the greatness of Einstein that he immediately understood the significance of Bose's leap of imagination, translated the paper into German and forwarded it to *Zeitschrift fuer Physik* with

2. VII, 24

Lieber. Herr Kollege!

Ich habe ihre Arbeit über-
-setzt und der Zeitschrift für
Physik zum Druck übergeben.
Sie bedeutet einen wichtigen
Fortschritt und hat mir
sehr gut gefallen. Ihre
Einwände gegen meine Arbeit
finde ich zwar nicht richtig.
Denn das Wien'sche Ver-
schiebungsgesetz setzt die
undulations theorie nicht voraus
und das Bohr.che korrespondenz-
prinzip ist überhaupt nicht
verwandt. Doch dies thut
nichts. Sie haben als erster
den Faktor quantentheoretisch
abgeleitet wenn auch wegen:
des Polarisations. Faktors 2
nicht ganz streng. Es ist
ein schöner Fortschritt.

Mit freundlichen Gruss
(L) Ihr A Einstein.

Postcard from Einstein, 2nd July, 1924

his own recommendation. He also sent a postcard to Bose acknowledging the paper and its great significance. The paper was subsequently published in the September 1924 issue of the journal.

What is the scientific significance of Bose's small paper? It is said that even Einstein did not fully understand its implications until much later when other physicists did further research on its basis. Actually, Bose's assumptions and mathematical tools turned out to be suitable for determining the energy of any system at a particular temperature. Now, a system—whether it is a gas, water vapour or radiation—is composed of several particles with varying energies at that temperature. To determine the energy distribution of a system at a specific temperature, one has to use the mathematical method or tool for counting the large number of particles it is composed of, called 'statistics'.

For counting the particles, Bose's first important step was to assume radiation to be a gas of photons. Secondly, he assumed them to be identical, a novel concept then, with wider implications in any system. Thirdly, he assumed them to be having the same energy level or state—again, an intuitive assumption which later proved to be correct. These assumptions may sound simple but they have deep roots in modern physics as it was found later.

Now, to count these particles and then to sum up their energies for a system at a specific temperature, Bose had to resort to what is known as 'Permutation and Combination'. Just as in a group photograph, all the persons can be photographed together in many different ways, these particles were counted in as many ways to give the energy distribution of the system.

This method of counting particles with aforementioned assumptions—now became 'rules' of nature and is now called 'Bose Statistics' (or 'Bose-Einstein Statistics') and the elementary particles, like photons, which obey these 'rules', are called 'Bosons'. In due course, following the footsteps of Bose, the British physicist P. A. M. Dirac and the Italian-American physicist Enrico Fermi independently showed that some other particles, namely, electrons, follow a different set of rules. Those particles are called 'Fermions' and the method of counting that they follow is called 'Fermi-Dirac Statistics'. Today, it has been found that elementary particles like photons, mesons, etc. swamp half the universe. That is why half the universe is 'Bosons'!

'Quantum Statistical Mechanics' determines the most probable behaviour of a system consisting of an assembly of quantum particles such as photons, at a specific temperature. Even before the subject of 'Quantum Mechanics', which determines energy of a system, gained

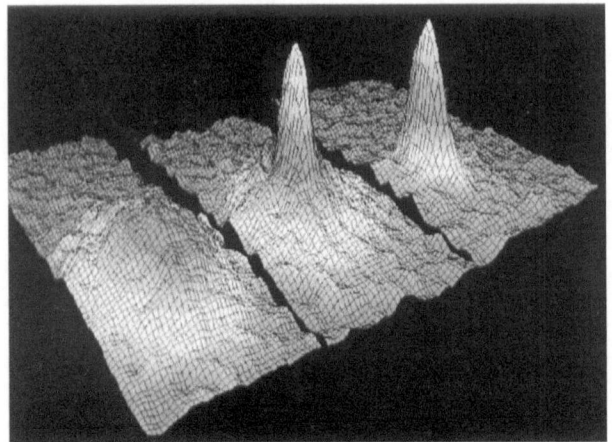

Bose-Einstein Condensate experimentally observed. These three images depict the various states of a Bose-Einstein Condensate–just before its appearance (left), just after its appearance (middle) and after further evaporation (right) leaving a sample of nearly pure condensate.

firm ground, Bose laid the foundation of the more advanced Quantum Statistical Mechanics due to his intuitive assumptions and rules. His work also led to the emergence of what is today known as the 'Quantum Field Theory' or 'Quantum Electrodynamics', which deals with emission and absorption of elementary particles. It is even claimed that Bose intuitively discovered the very important concept of 'spin' of an elementary particle in the same paper. In fact, his work became the crucial link between the old quantum theories of Max Planck,

Niels Bohr and Albert Einstein and the new quantum mechanics of Erwin Schroedinger, Werner Heisenberg, P. A. M. Dirac, Wolfgang Pauli and Max Born.

Later, Einstein went on to show that Bose's statistics applied to gases leads to the creation of a novel state at absolute zero degree Kelvin temperature (-273 degree Celisus), called 'Bose-Einstein Condensation'. This state is called so because when a gas is cooled its droplets condense to form a liquid. In 1994, such a novel state, when the atoms of a gas were stimulated to 'flock together and sing in unison', was independently created in two U.S. laboratories. The state was such a scientific curiosity, with considerable applications in the emerging technology at an extremely micro level—nanotechnology—that the 2001 Nobel Prize was awarded to its three American creators, Eric A. Cornell, Carl E. Wieman and Wolfgang Ketterle. Earlier, the possibility of the existence of such a state became evident from the discoveries of 'Superconductivity' and 'Superfluidity', when some materials were found to assume zero electrical resistance and zero viscosity respectively at extremely low temperatures.

In the eleven days after sending his first paper to Einstein, Bose investigated the same subject in further detail and wrote another paper 'Thermal Equilibrium in Radiation Field in Presence of Matter'. He again sent this second paper to Einstein but this time the response was not so warm. Although Einstein translated the paper into German and sent it to the journal he added a short note criticising certain aspects of Bose's findings.

Meanwhile Bose had been making efforts to visit Europe, meet top scientists and work in their laboratories. But he was not given the necessary funds to do so as the Dhaka University was then facing a financial crunch. It was only when Bose showed Einstein's postcard praising his contributions to the concerned authorities that the University granted him a two year study leave for Europe! He even received a visa for Germany immediately after he showed the same post card to the German Embassy!

In September 1924, Bose set sail for Paris from Mumbai. He selected the French capital as his first destination because he was quite conversant with French language and literature. He stayed at India House and through some friends there he was introduced to the eminent French physicist Paul Langevin. He was then working in Madame Curie's famous laboratory in the Municipal School where radium was discovered. Langevin introduced Bose to Madame Curie. But when she insisted that Bose should first learn French before joining her laboratory, as she already had problems with another Indian who did not know French, Bose simply kept quiet and left.

Marie and Pierre Curie in their laboratory and Paul Langevin

Why Bose did not tell her that he already knew French, is one of the mysteries of his character. Quite likely, he had changed his mind after meeting the legendary figure and seeing her laboratory. Subsequently, he was introduced to another eminent French physicist, Maurice De Broglie who was a X-ray crystallographer. For the next few months, Bose worked in his laboratory and learnt the basics of how X-rays could be used to reveal the internal arrangement of crystals and chemical compounds. It is quite likely that he felt he should learn something which would be of practical value to his countrymen. After returning home, he did set up a

Fritz Haber, Otto Hahn, Lise Meitner and Hans Geiger

well equipped X-ray crystallography laboratory at Dhaka University and trained several students in this novel technique to unravel the internal structure of crystals.

From Paris, Bose went to Berlin with his long cherished dream of doing research under the guidance of Einstein, whom he considered his guru. During those days, Berlin was a major centre of scientific research in the world, where several eminent physicists, such as Fritz Haber, Otto Hahn, Lise Meitner, Wolfgang Pauli, Werner Heisenberg and Hans Geiger were engaged in frontline scientific studies. Apart from rubbing shoulders with these giants of science, many of whom won the Nobel Prize later, Bose could finally meet and work with Einstein.

In the very first meeting, Einstein enquired how Bose had arrived at those assumptions or rules mentioned in his paper. Unfortunately, nothing much is known about how things went on between the two so far as research was concerned because Bose never talked about it. Quite likely, Bose left Einstein as a disappointed man. He never even talked about the third research paper which he had sent to Einstein on the subject of radiation when he was in Paris. What is even more surprising is that no record of this paper exists today as Bose did not keep a duplicate copy. The only record of the existence of this paper is to be found in his discussion about it with Langevin who had found it quite interesting.

It is quite likely that when Bose met Einstein, the latter's interest had already shifted to other frontier fields in physics and may be, he had given a cold reception to Bose's ideas in the second and third papers. Nevertheless, Einstein's letters of recommendation did open several doors for Bose and he met several eminent German physicists, visited major libraries and laboratories. But, strangely enough, throughout these two years in Europe, he did not write or get published a single research paper in modern physics, when his own contributions had triggered off such rapid developments in it.

Moreover, now it appears as though Bose had given up his specialised field of research because he did not produce a single paper in it even after his return to India. It is said that he was disappointed at Einstein's criticism on his second paper which he personally considered to be a far more significant work than the first one. However, later, in 1955, he was eagerly waiting to meet Einstein at Bern, Switzerland, where 50 years of his Theory of Relativity were to be celebrated. Here he came to know of the death of Einstein and wept bitterly.

After his return to Dhaka University in 1926, Bose took up experimental researches in physics more seriously. He began to set up facilities in the physics department for researches in X-ray crystallography, magnetic properties of matter, spectroscopy and the Raman effect. A workshop necessary for repair and maintenance of instruments and a well-stocked library containing the latest books and research publications were also established by him in the Department. Under his guidance, some special equipment were designed and built and he initiated research in statistics.

For the next eighteen years while he was in Dhaka, Bose was totally devoted to his students and their research work. He created the right intellectual environment for the cultivation of scientific attitude and research in his Department. His door was always open to his students and anybody could enter his room at any time. He also conducted informal classes, which often comprised 9-10 graduate or post-graduate students and the lectures had no barriers of time. A chain smoker, he always carried a sandalwood box of cigarettes to class. His students even had the liberty to take these cigarettes, provided some were left for him.

Unlike most senior researchers, Bose never asked his students to perform calculations for his personal research. Instead he would try to solve any problems, even personal and domestic ones that were brought to him by his students. Whenever any eminent contemporary scientist, like C. V. Raman, Meghnad Saha, S. K. Mitra or D. M. Bose, came to visit the Department he would take the opportunity to have their lectures arranged for students so that they were made aware of the latest developments in the subject. Moreover, Bose was not only interested in problems in physics; he was equally interested in mathematics, botany and chemistry. Often, teachers, researchers and students from other departments came to consult him on research problems related to their subjects. Moreover, he was never in a race to publish research papers and did not believe in the prevailing 'publish or perish' syndrome that continues to bog down scientific research even today. In fact, he used to urge his students not to give importance to marks, number of research papers or degrees. He always laid stress upon understanding science and doing quality research. He believed that the best way to understand an equipment was to build it with one's own hands.

Bose always urged students to start any work from the fundamentals and always read the masters in the field. He himself did not try to secure a Ph.D. degree,

At the National Physical Laboratory. Seated (left to right): A. P. Mitra, A. R. Verma, S. N. Bose, T. V. Ramamurty. Standing (left to right): Premprakash, V. G. Bhide, G. C. Jain, F. C. Auluck

though later he received honarary degrees from several Indian universities. Among his well known students were R. C. Majumdar, S. R. Khastgir, K. Banerjee and Abdul Matin Chaudhuri.

The lack of a Ph.D. degree created considerable problems for Bose when he applied for Professorship at the Dhaka University. On the suggestion of his friends, he requested Einstein, Langevin and others to support his candidature for the post by sending the necessary recommendations to the University. In this manner, he became Professor and, subsequently, the Provost of Dacca Hall and the Dean of the Faculty of Science.

Under normal circumstances, Bose would not have liked to leave Dhaka University as he himself had set up the Physics Department and had a large following among students and colleagues. Those were the 'happiest' days of his life. His home had a beautiful spacious garden, where he used to lie with a book and read. But Independence of India was round the corner. The Muslim political parties of East Bengal were demanding a separate state. Off and on, communal riots were breaking out in different parts of East Bengal and in Dhaka. It was with considerable reluctance that in 1945 Bose agreed to join his alma mater as the Khaira Professor of Physics in Calcutta University's College of Science, though earlier he had declined the offer for the same post.

CHAPTER FOUR

HOMECOMING

B ose's return to Kolkata was heartily welcomed by his former colleagues, friends and students. At the University College of Science, he had the intellectual company of Saha who had returned from Allahabad University and Sisir K. Mitra, another upcoming Indian physicist, who had made pioneering studies in ionospheric and radio physics. Meanwhile the efforts of Raman in setting up a school of research in Kolkata were paying rich dividends. He had won the Nobel Prize in 1930 and then shifted to Bangalore. However his name still attracted a considerable number of bright students and researchers to the college from all parts of the country.

Meanwhile Bose's colleagues and former collegemates Saha and Mitra tried to set up their own schools of research and went on to set up a science base in the country. Saha set up the Saha Institute of Nuclear Physics and Mitra the Institute of Radio Physics and Electronics, both in Kolkata. Bose however, continued his life and research at his usual pace. He never bothered about developing his career as a research scientist or creating a new school of research. But, yes, he continued in his own small way by guiding students in various research fields which he thought were relevant to the needs of his countrymen.

Under his guidance, research work began at the college on the X-ray studies of various minerals, soils and shales found in different parts of the country. When he came to know that some hot springs in Bakreswar contained traces of Helium gas which has considerable importance in industries, he began its study and collection. In fact, under his supervision a laboratory was set up at Bakreswar. Under his guidance, a novel thermoluminescent analyser for studying various aspects of materials was also designed and fabricated. He also urged his students to look in various minerals for the newly discovered Germanium, which has now assumed considerable importance in the electronics industry. Moreover, he was keen to follow the footsteps of his father as well as his teacher P. C. Ray and hoped to synthesise and manufacture a drug which would be of use to the common man. He succeeded in synthesising a chemical which was sold as an 'eye drop' even after he passed away.

After 1951, Bose went abroad every year. It was however his trip to Tokyo, Japan, where he had gone to present a paper in a seminar on science education which proved an eye opener for him. He was amazed to find that in schools and colleges, the Japanese used their own language as a medium of communication in science while adopting English scientific words. Even in the seminar, where he had expected to hear English, various presentations were made in Japanese. Even several science journals were being published in Japanese. He then realised that a mother tongue could be—and should be—used as a means of teaching science. He rightly felt that as English was usually the medium of communication, non-English speaking students resorted to cramming their science books because they were unable to express themselves correctly in English. So, when he returned home, he began a crusade for the teaching of science in one's mother tongue.

Meanwhile India had gained Independence in 1947 and nationalistic feelings were at its peak. Bose and his like-minded friends decided to do something to encourage the communication of science through their mother tongue, Bengali. In 1948, they laid the foundation of the Bangiya Bigyan Parishad in Kolkata with Bose as its President. Among its several activities of bringing science to children and the masses through

Bengali, the Parishad brought out the monthly science magazine *Jyan-O-Bigyan* (Knowledge and Science) that was aimed at school-going children.

Earlier, in 1931, Bose had written his first article in Bengali titled 'Crisis in Science' for the *Parichay* magazine. Now he became very active in propagating science through Bengali and this he continued to do till his death. He not only wrote popular science articles but also began to give popular talks and lectures in Bengali. He even began to gave lectures on the frontiers of modern physics to post-graduate students in Bengali. His style of presentation, whether written or oral, was always colloquial and easily understood. He himself never wrote a book in Bengali but inspired several students and colleagues to write science text-books and popular science books.

Bose and Rabindranath Tagore never had a close relationship, though in his youth he was a part of the literary circle that had grown around the Tagore family. However Tagore had a high regard for his contributions to science. In fact, when he had met Einstein in Germany, he was impressed by the fact that the latter had enquired only about Bose. In 1937, when Tagore wrote his only book on the universe titled *Visva Parichay* he dedicated it to Bose. Tagore died in 1941 but it was not a surprise, when in 1956, Bose was invited to become the Vice

Albert Einstein and Rabindranath Tagore

Chancellor of Viswa Bharati University which Tagore had established at Santiniketan, near Kolkata.

Bose readily agreed to assume this prestigious position because he knew of the ideals of Tagore and what he sought to achieve through his university. So, from the first day of joining the university, he set upon himself the task of reinforcing the ideals of Tagore which he thought had been lost sight of after his death. For instance, he was keen on an informal relationship between the teacher and the taught, a system that he practised himself. He was keen on an integrated education that would produce a truly cultured alumni. He was particularly keen to give more importance to science at various levels because it had become an integral part of life.

Bose was interested in introducing post-graduate classes in science and to set up an Advanced Centre of Science at Santiniketan. He was also eager to convert a meditation centre, which was used only once a week, into a reading room. He had ambitious plans of setting up a biogas plant in the campus so that it could be used to produce gas for the school laboratories. He also discovered that all outdoor classes were cancelled whenever there was rain. He gradually realised that the university staff had turned Tagore's ideals into fixed, ritualistic rules to be followed blindly and were against any change. He became frustrated and disillusioned as he had joined the university with the fervent hope of introducing some educational values which had always been in his mind.

Bose felt relieved when on his retirement from the Viswa Bharati University in 1957, he was made an Emeritus Professor at Calcutta University and two years later a National Professor. He was given some funds and facilities to conduct any research that he wanted but by then he was a disillusioned and disappointed man. Earlier, the Department of Physics of Dhaka University, for the establishment of which he had worked hard and selflessly, had been lost to him when Dhaka became a

On the dais with Neils Bohr

part of East Pakistan (now Bangladesh). Then several of his former East Bengali friends, colleagues and students flocked to West Bengal and Kolkata as refugees, penniless and homeless.

Though disillusioned personally, Bose was however receiving accolade after accolade when India gained Independence. During 1945–48, he became the President of the reputed Indian Physical Society; during 1948–50, he became the President of the prestigious National Institute of Science (now Indian National Science Academy) and earlier, in 1944, he had become the President of the well known Indian Science Congress. In 1954, he was bestowed with a Padma Vibhushan. He was also nominated for the Rajya Sabha in the same year.

Several Indian universities showered honorary doctorates upon him. Even Viswa Bharati honoured him with the Deshikottama Award in 1961.

To top it all, in 1958, Bose was elected a Fellow of the prestigious Royal Society of London, an honour which was long overdue. During those days, several top physicists, like P. A. M. Dirac, Niels Bohr and J. D. Bernal, visited Kolkata and met him. He also went abroad as a delegate to various international conferences and seminars, met several eminent physicists and exchanged ideas and views.

On his eightieth birthday, an international seminar was held in Kolkata to celebrate 50 years of his immortal discovery. Eminent scientists from all over the world came to attend the seminar. Bose, old and tired, could not stand up for long to address the audience and gave the address while seated. In the speech he said that he had been paid his due for his discovery and had therefore no desire to live any more. One month later, on February 4, 1974, he passed away at his own house in Kolkata. He left practically nothing for his surviving wife, two sons and five daughters. On the day of his death, students put on badges in Bengali that said 'Our Homage to the Undying Lamp' and came to pay their last homage to the great physicist and teacher.

A scientist is often free from emotions and feelings because he or she gets into the habit of viewing the world objectively. Moreover, he is so engrossed or obsessed by his research that he often has no time for anything which does not concern his field of research. Besides, if he is ambitious, as modern scientists often are—he is always trying his best to get as many research papers published as possible and have as many students to do research under his guidance. He is always applying and lobbying for funds for his research work and even hobnobing with powerful scientist-bureaucrats or politicians with an eye on big posts, projects and awards.

Bose had none of these qualities of a modern scientist. He never even bothered to keep track of his observations and researches not to speak of research papers. Once his work was done and he himself was satisfied, he would throw away all the loose sheets. Throughout his life, he wrote only 25 research papers and hardly 12 students did Ph.D. under his guidance. One can imagine how little his concern was for his career from the simple fact that he never submitted a thesis to any university for a Ph.D. degree. He had therefore to seek letters of recommendations from Einstein and others to convince the university authorities about the worth of his scientific contributions. Strangely enough, Einstein, Dirac and Fermi went on to be honoured with the Nobel Prize but not Bose though he was nominated for it.

Singer friend Dilip Kumar Roy

In short, Bose was beyond classification because physics and mathematics were just one of his interests. He was as much interested in music, literature and fine arts. If invited, he would never miss a musical concert or soiree or an art exhibition. Whenever his singer friend Dilip Kumar Roy came to visit him in Dhaka, they used to search for the houses of expert musicians, the *ustads*, to listen to their concerts. Also, whenever Roy visited him in Dhaka, Bose would organise his musical programmes and invite friends, colleagues and students. In fact, he himself was an adept *Esraj* and flute-player and would play them for friends.

Bose was extremely fond of French literature and even translated some famous French short stories into Bengali. In addition to English and Bengali, he was equally at home in German and Sanskrit. When once somebody asked him why he read so much, he countered by asking, why did he eat so much. Much talked about was his habit of apparently 'dozing off during musical concerts or even science lectures. But when they were over, he would open his eyes and ask some very pertinent and incisive questions.

Bose also loved good clothes and was fond of wearing the typical Indian dress *churidar kurta-pyjama* with a long overcoat. He also liked wearing woollen caps and had a good collection of caps and walking sticks.

In short, Bose looked at the world in totality and believed in enjoying his life fully. He was a true man of the proverbial 'Two Cultures', namely, sciences and humanities. But he was also a blend of the orient endowed with the temper of a visionary and the occident, a true man of the world. He did not have the one-track mind of a scientist who was keen to excel in his field of research and win accolades and honours from his fellow scientists. In fact, he never did anything in a calculated manner to win prestige or power.

Of course, Bose needed some strong provocation or challenge to do research in any field. But once his interest was aroused he would not give it up until the problem was solved to his satisfaction. For lack of inspiration he did not touch the subject of radiation again after his return from Europe. Thirty years later, the Unified Field Theory, which dealt with the unification of four forces of natures, namely, gravitation, electromagnetism, short-range and long-range nuclear forces, drew his attention during the

Indian Science Congress held in Kolkata. He then went on to write three excellent research papers between 1953 and 1956. Einstein was absolutely right when he called him 'a man of unusual gift and depth'.

Besides, Bose's range of interest was also wide. He did research in as diverse fields as X-ray crystallography, organic chemistry, ionosphere, geology, archaeology, mathematics and statistics. His depth of knowledge in other fields, such as, music and language, was considerable. Even his suggestions and criticisms in music and the Bengali language were duly taken by his friends when they wrote authoritative books on these subjects.

Strange enough, though his immortal work was purely mathematical, Bose laid immense stress upon experimental research among his students as he felt it was of considerable benefit to his countrymen. Had he concentrated on his main field with sustained efforts and zeal and produced a few more remarkable papers in modern physics, the Nobel Prize would have been his.

Bose had the prodigious mental abilities of a first-rate scientist but he also possessed a deeply compassionate nature like Lord Buddha whom he admired. Once during his childhood he gave his own food to a hungry street urchin and went hungry himself. Later, he freely gave his time to his friends, colleagues and students to solve their scientific problems. If the situation demanded, he would even listen to their domestic problems and solve them if he could. Although he did not participate much in the debates and discussions in the Rajya Sabha, when he was its member for five years, his compassionate nature did take up the cause of resettlement of Bengal refugees after Saha passed away.

In fact, Bose's personal philosophy was that life was for making friends and he did his utmost to maintain his friendships, whether he was in Kolkata, Dhaka, Paris or Tokyo. As a result, he was a highly social person. Moreover, he believed that when ideas are talked, discussed and debated, they get transformed and concretised in the mind. From his childhood, he loved what is popular in Bengal as *adda*—talking with friends on any subject under the sun without any direction or purpose over a cup of tea, snacks and Bengal grams. He had the habit of speaking authoritively on any subject— whether pickle-making or the pre-French Revolution conditions—except science. In fact, the eminent chemist P. C. Ray often referred to him as the prime example of his pet theory of a 'Bengali misusing his brain'.

Although Bose knew this weakness, he never regretted it or made any effort to curb it. In fact, as he grew old, he became more fond of *addas*. During his youth, he used to regularly visit his friends staying in distant parts of Kolkata for sessions of *adda*. But when he grew old and

Bose playing the Esraj for the Mahalanabises on the occasion of a wedding anniversary

it became difficult to walk, his own bedroom, which was always in disorder—crammed with books, newspapers, and cats—became the centre of *adda*. His favourites—a vase of flowers, an ashtray and a box full of cigarettes—were also his constant companions in those days. In fact, he was often called the 'King of Addas'. Despite this casual exterior which gave him the image of a 'spoilt genius', Bose continued his research work till the end of his life. Even when he passed away, he left behind some unfinished jottings on the theory of numbers which had aroused his interest while teaching mathematics to his daughter.

To sum up, Bose was a true renaissance man and he was very aware of his social responsibility to people and to his country and tried his best to achieve whatever little he could. His efforts to popularise science in his mother tongue and his emphasis on experimental research to produce something of worth to the common man are to be appreciated even today when modern Indian scientists are still in the rat race to win accolades abroad rather than do something worthwhile for their countrymen. Bose rightly assessed himself when he said, 'I was like a comet, a comet which came once and never returned again'. We are all awaiting the arrival of another such comet on the firmament of Indian Science.

SAYINGS OF S. N. BOSE

No difficulty is insurmountable to persistent and consistent endeavour.

Never accept an idea as long as you yourself are not satisfied.

Study the masters! Science, divorced from pragmatic considerations, is even worse than speculative philosophy.

We should never really be ashamed of going down to the mines, factories and railway lines to finish our scientific training, nor should industry fight shy of our universities on the false ground that they produce only theoretical and academic men.

Every true scientist who engages in research not merely for his self-satisfaction or egotism dreams all the time that he might discover some fundamental principle that will help us build a monument to human progress.

CHRONOLOGY

1894   Born on January 1, in Kolkata

1907   Joins Hindu School, Kolkata

1909   Stands fifth in the order of merit in the Entrance Examination of Calcutta University; joins Presidency College

1913   Stands first in B.Sc. with honours in mixed mathematics

1914   Marries 11-year-old Ushabati Ghosh

1915   Stands first in M.Sc. in mixed mathematics

1917   Joins as Lecturer at the University College of Science

1919   First research papers in mathematics published; joint research paper with Meghnad Saha; translates Einstein's Theory of Relativity with Saha into English

1921   Joins Dhaka University, Dhaka, (now in Bangladesh) as Reader in the Department of Physics

1924   Sends his immortal paper 'Planck's Law and the Light Quantum Hypothesis' to Albert Einstein; it was published in *Zeitschrift fur Physik;* leaves Mumbai by ship to Paris

1926   Returns to India and appointed Professor at Dhaka University on Einstein's letter of recommendation

1945   Joins Calcutta University, as Khaira Professor of Physics and becomes President of Indian Physical Society

1948   Launches *Bangiya Bigyan Parishad* for popularising science through Bengali; becomes President of the National Institute of Sciences (Indian National Science Academy)

1954   Honoured with the Padma Vibhushan; nominated to the Rajya Sabha

1956   Becomes Vice Chancellor, Viswa Bharati University, Santiniketan

1957   Elected a Fellow of the Royal Society, London;
       nominated Professor Emeritus at Calcutta
       University

1959   Appointed National Professor; resigned from
       Rajya Sabha

1974   Eightieth birthday celebrated all over India; dies
       on February 4 in Kolkata.

BIBLIOGRAPHY

Singh, Jagjit, *Some Eminent Indian Scientists,* Publications Division, 1966.

Special Issue on S. N. Bose, *Science Today,* July 1974.

Chatterjee, Santimay and Chatterjee, Enakshi, *Satyendranath Bose,* National Book Trust, 1976.

S. N. Bose: The Man and His Work Part I and Part II, S. N. Bose National Centre for Basic Sciences, 1994.

Satyendranath Bose—A Centenary Tribute, The Asiatic Society, 1995.

Special Issue on Satyendranath Bose, The Asiatic Society Vol XXXVI (4), 1995.

G. Venkataraman, *Bose and his Statistics,* Universities Press, 1996

ACKNOWLEDGEMETS

I am thankful to Dr M. C. Jain of Hindu College, Delhi, and Dr S. N. Ekbote of National Physical Laboratory, New Delhi, for going through the manuscript and suggesting changes. Thanks are also due to the Director, S. N. Bose National Centre for Basic Sciences, Kolkata, for the photographs published in this book.